TIME TRAVEL
AT
Puddle Lane

Time Travel at Puddle Lane

Emma Shevah
Illustrated by Laura Catalán

BLOOMSBURY EDUCATION
LONDON OXFORD NEW YORK NEW DELHI SYDNEY

BLOOMSBURY EDUCATION
Bloomsbury Publishing Plc
50 Bedford Square, London, WC1B 3DP, UK
29 Earlsfort Terrace, Dublin 2, Ireland

BLOOMSBURY, BLOOMSBURY EDUCATION and the Diana logo are trademarks of
Bloomsbury Publishing Plc

First published in Great Britain in 2022 by Bloomsbury Publishing Plc

ISBN: PB: 978-1-8019-9139-1; ePDF: 978-1-8019-9137-7; ePub: 978-1-8019-9138-4

2 4 6 8 10 9 7 5 3 1

Text design by Sarah Malley

Printed and bound in the UK by CPI Group Ltd, CR0 4YY

To find out more about our authors and books visit www.bloomsbury.com
and sign up for our newsletters

CONTENTS

Chapter One   7

Chapter Two   16

Chapter Three   25

Chapter Four   36

Chapter Five   44

Chapter Six   51

Chapter Seven   59

Chapter Eight   66

CHAPTER ONE
THE LIBRARY DOOR

Ariella and Yosef liked their school. They liked that it was called 'Puddle Lane School' because they liked the word 'puddle' and they very much liked puddles. They liked that it was in the heart of London, near the River Thames and Blackfriars Bridge. And they liked that it was a short walk from the sandy, beige dome of St Paul's Cathedral and the shiny Shard that tapers at the tip in a tall, split pyramid of glass.

As Yosef was interested in history, he was proud that his school was near the street where the Great Fire of London had started in a bakery in 1666. He loved that his school had an old, grand main building with high-ceilinged rooms and long windows, as well as a modern extension block housing classrooms, the gym and the library. And he liked that their teachers were kind (mainly), the lessons were fun (mainly), and there were four hamsters in Classroom 4 that the pupils could take turns to look after in the holidays.

As Ariella was interested in people, she liked that the streets on her way to school were full of adults wearing smart clothes and expensive-looking rucksacks, walking briskly, and holding paper coffee cups. She wondered what they did all day in the offices she could see from her classroom windows, and whether she would do whatever it was too when she was older. She liked learning in the happy, colourful classrooms, and she was especially fond of the portrait of the school's founder, Clara Conway, which hung above the reception desk.

The plaque underneath said that the portrait had been painted in 1846, which was so long ago that Ariella couldn't even imagine what her school or the world would have looked like back then. The portrait was as lifelike as a photograph, and Clara Conway seemed as real as if she were standing there in person. She was young and friendly-looking, with bright eyes full of determination and dark hair tied back in a bun. She leaned on a walking stick and wore a yellow and grey dress with a multitude of folds that Yosef said must have taken hours to paint.

In the 1840s, Clara Conway had established Puddle Lane School to provide an education for the poor boys and girls of the neighbourhood. She'd done it at a time when school education was mainly for the rich, and even then, almost entirely for boys. Although their school was for everyone now, if it weren't for Clara, Ariella and Yosef would have no reason to walk down Puddle Lane every day with their big brother Daniel, past the tall Monument that marked where the Great Fire had started all those years ago.

Every morning, when they walked through the main door into their school, Ariella and Yosef looked up at the portrait. "Thank you, Clara," Ariella often sang with a wave. "If it wasn't for her," she liked to remind Yosef, "this school wouldn't be here." And she was right.

Their favourite place at school was the library. It had reading nooks, beanbags and blankets, and books stacked on old wooden shelves. At the back of the library, a glass cabinet displayed archaeological relics that had been discovered when the builders had excavated the site to build the new block. There were about thirty objects in total, all labelled and roughly dated. The cabinet was always locked and the only person with the key was Miss Richie, the librarian, who was their favourite teacher of all.

Miss Richie used to wear wacky clothes that never seemed to match – a pink t-shirt with yellow checked trousers and a purple cardigan one day, a blue flowery dress with orange tights and a teal jumper another day – but lately, she had only worn dark colours, ankle-length skirts and long sleeves. Her once light-pink hair was now as brown as the fur on Bruno the hamster in Classroom 4. No one knew why Miss Richie's appearance had changed so drastically, but Ariella and Yosef were relieved that her personality hadn't changed because she was warm and funny, and she always made them feel welcome in the library.

One Monday at break, Yosef was wedged in a beanbag gazing at black-and-white photographs of Hyde Park in the 1880s. Boys in suits and caps walked between men wearing top hats, women in long, full skirts and hats with big ribbons, and girls in white dresses with sashes. Yosef was trying to imagine being there with them, but some Year 6 girls were whispering and giggling, and he glanced at them in annoyance.

A long skirt suddenly blocked his view. "Which era this time?" Miss Richie asked, bending down to peer at him, her smile forming a dimple on her right cheek.

Yosef smiled and showed her the cover. "It's called *A Hundred Years Ago: Britain in the 1880s* but the 1880s aren't a hundred years ago," he frowned.

"Old book," Miss Richie replied, "but the photos are accurate." She glanced at the whispering girls. "Are they disturbing you?"

Yosef nodded.

"Well, we can't have that now, can we?" Miss Richie replied, standing up. She said to the girls in a cheerful tone, "Lovelies, this is the library. If you aren't here to enjoy the calm gift of reading, then please take your conversation to the playground."

The girls apologised and left, leaving the library wonderfully quiet. So quiet in fact that Yosef, who was tired because they'd been up late the night before celebrating Ariella's bat mitzvah, felt his eyelids droop heavier and heavier until he fell asleep.

He woke up suddenly when he heard a door open, a roar of noise, then silence as the door closed again.

Yosef sat up, rubbing his eyes. The library was empty. Not even Miss Richie was there. He glanced at the clock. Break had finished ten minutes ago – he was late for his lesson!

Suddenly, the door at the back of the library opened and Miss Richie walked in with soot on her dress and her face, and very black fingernails.

Yosef ducked under the blanket. He didn't want her to know he'd fallen asleep because she might not let him come back tomorrow. But he was curious, too, so he peeked out. Miss Richie's cheeks were red and she seemed flustered. She checked the cabinet, then walked over to the toilet, locking the door behind her.

This was his chance. Yosef rushed out of the library just as the teaching assistant, Miss Harrington, arrived looking frantic.

"There you are!" Miss Harrington said, crossly. "We were worried!"

"Sorry," Yosef answered. "I fell asleep."

CHAPTER TWO
RELICS OF LONDON

"That *is* odd," Ariella said when Yosef told her about Miss Richie on the way home. "Why would she be sooty with dirty fingernails?" Ariella's eyes scanned the tall buildings near their school. None of them had any chimneys.

"I don't know," Yosef replied. "But it must have something to do with the objects in the cabinet because she checked them as soon as she came back."

"Hmm." Ariella couldn't see the link, but as they walked, they devised a plan.

The next day at break, Ariella and Yosef looked more closely at the cabinet. The objects were organised chronologically, with the oldest (a stone tool from the Bronze Age, a Viking earring, a jewelled brooch and a Roman helmet) on the bottom shelf, and the newest (a medicine bottle from the 1800s, a fountain pen from 1910, and a notebook found in the Blitz) at the top. Miss Richie appeared behind them, her skirt swishing. "Fascinating, aren't they?" she murmured. "Relics of London history, and all found right here on the school site when they were building this new block."

Yosef pointed to a rectangular blue-and-white soap dish with holes at the bottom. Beside it was a label saying '**Circa 1820: Pearlware**'.

He knew that '*circa*' meant 'around about that time', and he thought that 1795 to 1837 was a specific era because he'd read about it and had an excellent memory for dates.

"Do you think it's really from the Regency era?" he asked Miss Richie.

"Absolutely," she replied with a smile. "I'm impressed. You're quite the historian."

Yosef swelled with delight, but before he could ask how archaeologists could be certain, Ariella pointed to the door at the back of the library. "Miss Richie?" she asked, "what's behind that door?"

"Narnia," Miss Richie replied with a wink. Then she added, "actually, it's a storeroom, but that's a boring answer." Pupils were lining up to take books out so Miss Richie returned to her desk.

"It can't be a storeroom," Yosef whispered to Ariella. "When she opened it, it was noisy, like she'd opened it onto a street."

"But… there's no street near this part of the school," Ariella said, glancing at Miss Richie. "What's she hiding?"

"No idea," Yosef replied. "But I'm desperate to find out."

"Me too. And if she won't tell us the truth, we'll have to find out for ourselves."

At break the following day, Ariella and Yosef watched Miss Richie carefully. She was being her usual merry self, but her drastic change of dress seemed more mysterious now.

At the end of break, Ariella hid behind the non-fiction shelves and Yosef reluctantly went to lessons to avoid getting into trouble. When she no longer heard footsteps, Ariella peeked out just enough to see.

Sure enough, when Miss Richie thought the library was empty, she scurried to the front door, twisted the sign so it read '**LIBRARY CLOSED**', and then opened her desk drawer. She lifted out a pencil case, removed some keys, and hurried to the cabinet, checking behind her that no one was watching. With the smaller key, she unlocked the glass door and took out a cowbell. She locked the cabinet, glanced around again, and then used the larger key to unlock the back door of the library. Ariella watched, bewildered, as Miss Richie stepped out and closed the door behind her. Ariella was sure she could hear mooing.

Ariella waited, her heart beating hard. She was late for her lesson and she'd be in trouble, but she had an excuse ready. When the door opened again and Miss Richie walked in, she had straw in her tangled hair, dirt smears on her cheek and a chicken feather on her sleeve. She brushed herself off, hurried to the small library toilet and closed the door.

Ariella heard the taps running and jumped up. She hurried to her classroom, telling her teacher she'd stayed in the library because she had a tummy ache.

*

"Something strange is going on," Ariella said to Yosef at lunchtime.

Yosef nodded. "Is the cowbell still in the cabinet?"

"Oh. I didn't check," Ariella said. "You're smart, little brother. Let's go and see at last break."

By then, Miss Richie was clean again. No straw, no tangled hair, no dirt smears, no chicken feathers. No one would have known if Ariella hadn't seen it with her own eyes.

Miss Richie was stamping return dates on books, recommending her favourite reads and being her usual friendly self. Ariella and Yosef smiled at her and casually walked over to the cabinet. The cowbell, *circa* 1140, was sitting on the middle shelf, where it was supposed to be.

"She takes something from the cabinet before she goes through the door," Yosef whispered. "I think we need to take an object out and go through that door ourselves."

"I think you're right," Ariella replied. "And I know just the time to do it."

*

After school on Wednesdays, Ariella usually stayed late to play football, Yosef had guitar lessons, and when they went home, they always ate pizza. But that Wednesday, they told their activities teachers that they felt unwell and would wait in the library. Some older children were in there doing homework, and Miss Richie, who was on the phone, didn't notice Ariella and Yosef come in. They hid under blankets in the nook, which was harder with two. Ariella was sure they'd be caught, but half an hour later, Miss Richie asked everyone to leave, turned out the lights and left the library.

Ariella and Yosef lifted the blanket but then heard footsteps and gasped.

"Must be Terry!" Yosef whispered. Terry the caretaker walked around after school, moving furniture and making sure everything was where it should be.

Ariella and Yosef hid again and came out only when there was silence.

"I'll get the keys," Ariella mumbled. She cautiously lifted the blanket and headed to Miss Richie's desk. She removed the keys from the pencil case and quickly tiptoed over to where Yosef stood by the cabinet.

"What shall we take out?" he asked.

"Um... the soap dish?" Ariella suggested. "I mean, it doesn't really matter because we have no idea what's behind the door. Let's just take something and hurry up."

Yosef nodded and lifted out the soap dish. "You open the back door so I don't drop it," he said.

Ariella nodded and slipped the long key into the keyhole. "What if it *is* just a storeroom?" she asked.

"With street noises, soot and feathers?"

"True," Ariella replied. She took a deep breath. "Ready?"

"Ready," Yosef replied.

So Ariella turned the key.

CHAPTER THREE
BEHIND THE DOOR

The door opened onto a wide dirt track bustling with horse-drawn carriages. Moustachioed men in top hats walked arm in arm with women in fancy bonnets and long dresses. Boys in caps played games with pebbles, and girls in frocks played hopscotch. Cloth awnings stretched from wooden-fronted shops with hand-painted signs that sold all kinds of wares, from horseshoes on tables to ribbons in baskets to whole skinned pigs hanging in rows at the entrance.

Ariella froze. "What... just happened?" She turned to face the door they'd just walked through. It was rough and wooden, and belonged to a ramshackle shed. Panicking, she grabbed the handle, turned the rusty knob, and pushed and shoved, but the door was locked and wouldn't budge.

"Yosef, I can't open it!" she cried, and eyed the street in fright. The air was cold, and in the dim yellow glow, Ariella could see her breath. A smoking oil lamp overhead cast long shadows making people look menacingly tall and a small, mangy dog look like a demon greyhound.

"Where… are we?"

"Wo-ah," Yosef breathed, his eyes darting from unfamiliar sight to unfamiliar sight, taking in the rowdy, reeking hubbub of it all. Old leather shoes, rolls of cloth, hearty pies and steaming tea kettles were piled high on stall tables with wheels. Horses, lots of them, were snorting and neighing, their dung slapping the already dung-thick dirt track. The smell of manure and meat flesh and musty malodours he couldn't identify hit him all at once. "It's… London," he replied. "Look."

The glass skyscrapers were nowhere to be seen, but the beige dome of St Paul's and the spires of multiple churches were visible through the fog. The street looked a lot like Puddle Lane, but also completely different. "I think the question is *when* are we. Probably some time in the 1800s but I can't be sure."

"But how do we get home?" Ariella wiped her clammy hands on her jumper and tried to keep calm. The street looked like a film set or painting. Smoke rose from every chimney, thickening the fog. Smoke rose, too, from the blazing oil lamps and from fires in tin tubs lit for warmth and to keep the large kettles and soup pots hot. There were families sitting on street corners who looked like they needed hot baths and decent meals. A few begged for coins, their thin coats threadbare and their boots full of holes. A coating of soot lay on the buildings, the people, the road.

Without realising it, Ariella and Yosef had drawn a crowd. They certainly stood out:

Yosef in his hoodie and trainers; Ariella in her stripey jumper, leggings and skirt, which came to her knees. No one else had a skirt so short and she suddenly felt very uncomfortable. "They're all looking at us," she said with a gulp.

Yosef tugged her sleeve and said, "Let's go." They weaved through the people, many of whom smelled so strongly it was hard not to wince. When they passed obvious thieves loitering near doorways, Ariella tucked her new necklace into her shirt collar. Her lovely grandmother, Naomi, had given her a gold chain and tree of life pendant for her bat mitzvah, and Ariella treasured it more than any other gift.

She and Yosef slipped into a large shop lined with wooden shelves. Outside, a Punch and Judy show had drawn a crowd. Ariella couldn't understand why anyone liked it: the puppets hit each other with clubs, their voices harsh and screeching, and they were cruel even to the baby, but the crowd was laughing and at least it meant the attention was not on them.

"Yosef," Ariella hissed as they stood behind two older women buying hats. "What're we going to do? Is this where Miss Richie's been coming? How does she get back into the library? Because I'm not staying here forever. It's pizza night."

Yosef shrugged. "I don't know… but this is amazing!"

"It's not amazing! It's a disaster. It's…"

"It's got something to do with this," Yosef said, holding up the soap dish. "I bet you. I know it's scary to be here but it's also incredible, don't you think?"

"No, Yosef. I do not *think*."

"We probably need to find out where this belongs," Yosef said, "and then we can go home."

Ariella sighed. That made sense. "How, though? The door's locked!"

"I don't know but…"

"If you please, might I be of service?" A black

woman with kind eyes stood at a polite distance, trying not to stare at them. She wore a long brown dress and white apron. Her hair was tied in a bun and covered in a bonnet. The turbaned shopkeeper was busy with a customer but his suspicious eyes were on the three of them.

"Yes, please, you may, actually," Ariella said firmly, raising her voice when the audience outside roared with laughter. "I'm Ariella. This is my brother, Yosef. We're… lost."

"Delighted to make your acquaintance," the woman replied with a shy smile. "My name is Florence Woebegone and I have been... lost... myself. It would be an honour to assist you."

"You've been... *'lost'*?" Ariella asked, raising an eyebrow.

"Most certainly. I entered this world on a Caribbean sugar plantation in the year of our Lord 1798. My former owner sold me when I was twelve and I had to leave my beloved sister Mary to sail with my new master to London to be a maid and playmate for his daughter, Miss Lucy. When the good Lord took her soul three years later, her father changed my name from Conway to 'Woebegone' for my misfortune, and wanted to sell me on. But his brother, Mr Richard Conway, was very much against slavery so he took me in, gave me a home and found me employment with Mr Singh. For this reason, I will always assist those far from home."

Ariella was flabbergasted. She had learned about the slave trade at school but to hear Florence call someone her 'owner' and speak of being 'sold' was shocking. And the name 'Woebegone', meaning very sad, seemed entirely wrong for someone so cheerful. "That's awful – all of it!" Ariella cried. "But how lovely of you to want to help other people after all that."

"Yes," Yosef agreed. "How can children be bought and sold? And how can someone change your name like that?" He shook his head in disbelief. He had been busy calculating – Miss Florence looked about thirty and if she was born in 1798 then they must be in the 1820s – but then he realised something. "Mr Richard Conway?" Yosef asked. "Is he related to Clara Conway, by any chance?"

"Indeed – he is her father," Florence replied, and added, "Oh, poor Miss Clara!" Ariella's eyes widened. "Why? What's wrong with her?"

"A carriage wheel hit a large chisel on the road this morning. It rebounded and cut deep into her leg. I fear she may…"

"This *establishment*," Mr Singh shouted, "is not a coffee parlour where one may indulge in *idle conversation*. It is a *mercantile* store in which to *purchase goods*!"

"Miss Florence," Yosef said, looking at the shelves, "we need clothes. To move around more freely."

Ariella nodded. "Skirts tend to be shorter where we come from. Everyone's staring at my legs."

She fished in her pocket and held out her pocket money. Florence glanced at the pound coins and whispered, "Foreign money is not accepted here, but I have savings. I shall purchase your clothing."

"Oh, no," Ariella said. "We can't let you…"

"If we are not on this earth to help one another," Florence replied with a smile, "then I do not know what we *are* here for. Come, Miss Ariella, take this skirt and shawl. And for you, Master Yosef, a jacket and cap. Mr Singh, I shall settle my bill on the morrow."

"You're so kind," Ariella said in disbelief. "How will we ever repay you?"

"That is not necessary," Florence replied softly. "My savings are for me to sail to Jamaica to find my sister. I hope to buy her freedom and bring her here. I shall do it at a later date, that is all. The shop is closing soon and I shall be leaving in a few minutes. Allow me to accompany you. Where might you be going?"

"To meet Clara Conway," Ariella replied.

"Then that is easy," Florence said. "For I still reside in the Conway family home."

CHAPTER FOUR
THE CONWAYS' HOUSE

Ariella and Yosef followed Florence past flower sellers with baskets of roses and carnations, market sellers arranging their cabbages, pears, apples and reeking fish, and stray cats chasing rats along alleyways.

The people of London in the 1820s were much more diverse than they had thought. There were lots of black men, women and children going about their business. Some were obviously rich and wore fine clothes and top hats, while others were working or wearing servants' uniforms. Customers bought cloth from Chinese families in long silk robes with wide sleeves. Middle Eastern traders in colourful hats sold spices and flatbreads. Sikh men with turbans drank tea beside their carts, and Jewish families stood deep in conversation in doorways beside prams with large wheels. They weren't olive-skinned and dark-haired like Ariella and Yosef, whose family came from Yemen on one side and Morocco on the other. The men wore black suits and fur-rimmed hats, the women wore head scarves and they all had light hair and pale skin. As they spoke Yiddish, Ariella and Yosef thought they might be from Russia or Poland.

Ariella was also surprised by the noise. Wheels clattered, horses neighed and hawkers yelled and sang their wares and prices. A drunk carriage driver bellowed, accusing another of stealing. Every five steps or so, they heard street musicians: some were talented, but others were playing fiddles, hurdy-gurdies and tin whistles badly, and wailing like they had toothache. Near a gallows, the smell of cabbage from a soup kitchen mingled with the stench of sewage from cesspools, piles of rotting vegetables, blood and urine.

"Noisy," Ariella shouted above the din.

"Stinky," Yosef mouthed. They turned a corner and saw animals. "Why are cows and pigs tied up here?" Yosef asked Florence.

"We are nearing the meat market," Florence said. "Beware of the blood."

They sidestepped a large pool of it, watching butchers hack through carcasses and flies land on the fresh meat. A man wearing a top hat with a leather case by his feet was squeezing and inspecting a liver he'd picked up from a tray.

"That gentleman is Doctor Hurst," Florence explained, "the Conway family physician. No doubt he's on his way to tend to Miss Clara but purchasing organs on the way for his students to dissect in anatomy classes. I have seen him doing so on a number of occasions. We shall arrive before him."

It was only a short way but it took a while to walk it. Yosef narrowly avoided two young boys running after horses to scoop up their droppings, then yelled, "Get back!" when a plank fell from wooden scaffolding beams, bounced off a ladder and just missed Ariella. There were no pavements so the chaos of jostling and noise and choking dust from the endless construction of new buildings meant it was hard to notice things falling from above.

"Good job you have sharp eyes," Ariella said gratefully.

"Puddle Lane," Florence announced. Yosef was amazed to see a row of houses on the street, but it was still very much in the business district: they'd passed numerous counting houses containing bearded men peering at heavy books. And then they saw it. Puddle Lane School, but not as they knew it.

The main school building was quite clearly a family home. The long windows were framed with yellow curtains, and round shiny tables inside displayed large vases of flowers. The front door was made of dark wood. Under the heavy knocker was the number 12 in brass.

"This…" Ariella said, "…reminds me of home."

While Florence greeted a neighbour, Yosef straightened his cap and whispered, "That area we've just walked through is where the new block is. The meat market is where the new classrooms are. The shop where Florence works is the gym. The shed door must be exactly where the library is now."

"We shall enter through the servants' quarters," Florence said, pointing to a door in the basement where their school dining room was now.

Downstairs, they met a white maid in a black dress, white apron and mob cap over her blond hair. She looked about fourteen. "Evenin', Miss Florence. Evenin', Master and Miss. I 'eard footsteps, and thought you was Doctor Hurst."

"Good evening, Miss Elsie. These are my friends, Master Yosef and Miss Ariella. They come from a foreign land. Doctor Hurst will arrive shortly: he was purchasing organs from the butcher. How is Miss Conway?"

"Oh, she's in *awful* pain. That cut is terrible deep."

Ariella looked worriedly at Yosef.

"Lemme get you tea and some buns," Elsie added, leading them through the servants' quarters into the kitchen. "Mrs Barrow is a marvellous cook."

The kitchen was warmed by a large open fire over which three chickens were roasting on a spit. Shelves were lined with copper pots and pans gleaming like mirrors. A long table held trays of potatoes and carrots, baskets of bread and a dead unplucked swan, and on the floor a wooden tub was filled with pigs trotters, giblets and the ends of leeks and onions.

Mrs Barrow, a large, red-faced woman with shiny cheeks, offered them buns fresh from the oven and a mug of sweet tea. Although Ariella and Yosef were hungry, they politely said "No, thank you," to the buns in case they contained lard. They weren't allowed to eat lard because it was made from pork fat, which wasn't kosher.

"I'm making Miss Conway a soup," Mrs Barrow said, pointing to the wooden tub on the floor. "To get her strength up."

Ariella had thought the scraps were to be thrown away. She grimaced at Yosef and then asked Elsie, "Could we meet Miss Conway? It's important."

Elsie snorted. "Definitely not."

Ariella had to think quickly. "If we don't, she might die, and then you'd lose your job and wouldn't be able to stay here."

Elsie frowned. "Alright. You'll need to be quick before the doctor gets here. Follow me."

CHAPTER FIVE
CLARA CONWAY

Elsie led them up the servants' staircase. It was steep and narrow, and at the back of the house. At the top, she looked left and right, and listened intently. Then she beckoned them to follow and opened a door to a large, high-ceilinged bedroom that Ariella and Yosef recognised as the Year 6 classroom.

Clara Conway was lying on a brass four-poster bed. She looked very much like a girl-version of the woman in the portrait, but she was about ten, pale and crying. She looked at them in distress.

"Miss Conway, some visitors asked to see you. They said it was urgent."

"I cannot... speak... ," Clara groaned, pulling back the blanket that was covering her leg and unwrapping the soiled bandage. The cut was large and deep, and her leg was bloody and swollen. Underneath it were dirty blood-stained rags. "OWWW," she wailed.

"Miss Conway!" Ariella exclaimed, moving towards her. "You do a wonderful thing when you're older. You start an amazing school and..."

Elsie gasped. She snapped at Ariella, "Miss, what're you talking about?"

"What my sister means," Yosef said, frowning at Ariella, "is that you'll be fine, Miss Conway."

Noticing an enamel basin and water jug on a table, he carefully took the soap dish from under his jacket and asked, "Is this yours, by any chance?"

Clara shook her head and groaned in pain.

"We don't have no soap dishes like that," Elsie said. Yosef glanced at Ariella in bewilderment. What was the link then with the soap dish?

Just then, the doorbell rang. Elsie said, "Oh, Lord," and ran down the back stairs, leaving Ariella and Yosef in the room, unsure of what to do.

"We need to get out of here," Yosef hissed, tucking the soap dish into his jacket.

"Miss Conway," Ariella said, getting used to the 'Miss' and 'Master' thing now, "we're friends and we want to help. We'll be downstairs with Florence but if you need anything, just let Elsie know."

Clara breathed out with a moan and nodded.

As they tiptoed down the back staircase, they heard Doctor Hurst speaking gruffly to Elsie. Then a woman greeted him warmly and his manner changed.

"Mrs Conway," he said, "how is my patient?"

Ariella paused on the stairs. "Must be Clara's mother," she whispered to Yosef.

"Feverish, Doctor," Mrs Conway replied, "and in dreadful pain. Please save her. She is my only surviving child."

Ariella's eyes stretched wide. "She can't die from a leg wound, can she?"

Yosef nodded. "Medicine used to be terrible. Infections, gangrene…"

Having a brother who loved history meant Ariella knew about gangrene. Not that

47

she wanted to. Yosef had told her about it in detail one morning at breakfast and she'd shouted at him to shush because he was making her feel sick. "Doctors knew nothing about germs back then," he'd told her, "and gangrene spread quickly. They tried to stop it by amputating limbs – without anaesthetic – but because they didn't wash the knives or needles, and nurses often washed wounds with the same sponge and water they'd used for all the patients on the ward, people died from infections all the time."

Ariella had gone off her breakfast by then.

But now, having gone back in time, she realised that Yosef's knowledge was useful.

*

"I've got it!" Ariella said. "Give me the soap dish. You go downstairs…" And she told him exactly what to do.

As Mrs Conway led the doctor up the main stairs, Yosef scurried down the back stairs and Ariella tiptoed up to the bed. She placed the soap dish near the jug and basin, then, hearing footsteps, put her finger to her lips to silence Clara. Quickly, she jumped under the bed, covering herself with the valance sheet just in time.

The doctor put his case down with a thump. It was inches from Ariella's ear.

"Good afternoon, Clara," he said in a formal tone. "Rest assured, I shall stitch up your leg and all will be well."

From his bag he removed an apron covered in dried blood and pus. Ariella could see the hem of it. It was disgusting. She tried not to yelp. He'd just been touching raw meat and now he was going to examine an open wound on Clara's leg and sew it up! Clara could lose her leg if it got infected. Or her life. And if she did, there would be no Puddle Lane School.

The doctor pulled back Clara's blanket, said, "Ye-es, I see," and bent down to take out some instruments. Ariella could see dirty, blood-smeared hands reach into his case. The scalpel and needle he took out were encrusted with blood from previous patients.

Ariella tried not to squeal.

Yosef, Florence and Elsie had to hurry if they were to help Clara.

CHAPTER SIX
THE STITCHES

Clara Conway moaned and writhed in pain; Ariella felt her moving around above her. Just as Doctor Hurst said, "Keep still, now," there were footsteps on the stairs.

"If you please, Ma'am, Cook has sent Doctor Hurst some stew and a pot o' coffee," Elsie said awkwardly, walking in with a tray. "And it's cooled down a bit so he can eat it right away."

"Goodness, Elsie," Mrs Conway snapped, "this is hardly the time. Doctor Hurst is performing an important procedure."

"As you wish, Ma'am," Elsie said. "I'll just put the tray over 'ere, shall I?" She swiftly entered the room, ignoring Mrs Conway's protests that she should take it away. As she rushed in, she tripped on the edge of the rug, sending the contents of the tray flying over Doctor Hurst. The tray hit the floor with a bang and clatter that made Ariella jump and Clara groan.

"Foolish girl!" Doctor Hurst cried. "I am covered in stew and coffee!"

"*Elsie!* Whatever were you thinking?" Mrs Conway shouted, and began apologising to the doctor and trying to calm poor Clara.

Fearfully, Elsie glanced down at Ariella who was peeking out of the valance. Ariella nodded eagerly and pointed to the soap dish. Elsie shifted near it, slipped a bar of soap out from her apron pocket and placed it onto the soap dish. Moving away a step, she said, "Oh, I am terrible sorry. What a clumsy oaf I am! I'll get a clean apron from cook. And there's some soap 'ere for the good doctor to wash 'is hands and get the

stew off of him. He can wash his knives and needles, an' all."

"Well, at least you have *some* common sense, girl," Doctor Hurst said with exasperation. He removed his disgusting apron and washed his hands in the basin using the soap. Elsie scurried to the door, took a clean apron from Florence, who had appeared with it as if by magic, and handed it to Doctor Hurst. In the chaos, no one seemed to notice that Florence was already waiting with it.

Under the bed, Ariella sighed with relief. She knew that sterile conditions and antiseptic were best for stitching up wounds, but Doctor Hurst washing his hands with soap and water, and changing his blood and pus-covered apron, had to be better than nothing.

Yosef had done a great job, and so had Elsie, Florence and Mrs Barrow.

"Clara, bite on this," the doctor ordered. He must have put a cloth in her mouth because Clara's cries became muffled.

"Elsie, Florence, come," Mrs Conway said, and Ariella felt the mattress buckle as the three of them held Clara down. As Doctor Hurst stitched the wound in her leg, Clara wailed bitterly and jolted the bed a number of times. Ariella, lying under it, wished she didn't have to hear Clara in pain, and wanted to hold her hand. It was a wonder anyone had survived operations in those days, she thought, with no anaesthetic, and doctors' dirty hands, knives and needles.

Eventually, Doctor Hurst finished. He gave Clara medicine from a bottle with some dark liquid inside, and Elsie and Mrs Conway escorted him downstairs.

Florence pulled back the valance sheet and Ariella came out from under the bed.

Clara was shocked to see Ariella, but she was dazed, whimpering in pain and her eyes were cloudy from the medicine.

"Miss Conway, I hope you get better soon," Ariella said. "It's been amazing to meet you.

I just wish we'd been able to hang out when you weren't in agony."

"How... strangely... you speak," Clara whispered, her eyes closing.

Ariella pointed to the bed. "Miss Florence, would you take that dirty rag out from under her leg and put clean cloths under it every hour? You and Elsie will need to keep the stitches and the wound clean with warm water and salt, so she doesn't get an infection."

"I am not familiar with the meaning of this word," Florence replied, "but it is not necessary to ensure Miss Conway's leg is clean. Miasma is what makes one unwell, so we shall be sure to keep the windows tightly shut so she does not breathe in the night air."

Ariella shook her head. "Where I come from," she replied, "hardly anyone suffers or dies from stitches because it's well known that wounds need to be kept clean. I promise you, it's not because of the night air."

Florence nodded, but Ariella could see she wasn't convinced.

"Miss Florence," Ariella persisted, "will you promise to keep Miss Conway's leg and her bed covers as clean as you can, and wash your hands with soap before touching her leg?"

"I shall," Florence replied, "and I shall see that Elsie does the same. But we shall also keep the windows firmly closed, just to be sure."

Ariella smiled. "Good idea." Clara was dozing, but Ariella wished her a speedy recovery and added, "Miss Florence, before we leave, would you show me your room? If you wouldn't mind, I think I need to lie down for a minute to recover my strength."

Florence smiled. "Of course." She took Ariella up the back stairs to her room in the attic. It was small but cosy, with a brass bed, a trunk on the floor and a beautiful oil painting on the wall. Florence left, closing the door quietly.

Ariella didn't need to lie down and rest – she had another plan entirely. She sat on the bed and gazed at the painting. It showed a ship arriving at an island with palm trees on the shore. Ariella knew why it was there and wondered whether Florence would ever find her sister. She also wondered whether she and Yosef would be able to go home now, or if they'd be stuck in the past forever. She unclasped the gold chain and removed her tree of life necklace. She placed it under Florence's pillow and patted it. "This should help," she whispered.

Then she went downstairs to find Yosef.

CHAPTER SEVEN
THE SHED DOOR

"God give you good morrow, my masters. Past five o'clock and a fair evening!" a watchman cried.

Florence led Ariella and Yosef through the misty twilight. Shopkeepers were closing shutters, sweeping dusty paths with scratchy brooms, removing their wares from tables, and extinguishing fires. Maids wrung clothes in large wooden tubs, their hands red raw and their dresses wet. Sooty chimney sweeps gazed at bakers taking hot loaves from glowing ovens, and near a standpipe, a crowd queued with buckets and jars to collect water.

Through the alley, they caught a glimpse of the Thames. There were so many masts and sails, they looked like trees in a wood.

"Woah," Yosef said, "can we detour? Please – just for five minutes?"

He ran down to the waterside, and Ariella and Florence followed. The river was buzzing with activity. Schooners, sailing boats, cargo ships and rowing boats covered the surface of the Thames. The three of them stood beside huge coiled ropes and anchors, watching wooden boxes and barrels being heaved and rolled down a gang plank. Sailors on the ships' rigging shouted, and dockers unloaded goods into wooden warehouses. One docker slipped a packet into his coat and winked at Yosef.

Ariella gazed around and then gasped. There was an eerie space where Tower Bridge should have been. "Look!" she said to Yosef.

The only bridge they could see was old and wooden, and had shops and houses across it. "Must be the old London Bridge," he murmured.

"I wish I had a camera. I don't ever want to forget this," Yosef said.

"Imagine pulling out a phone," Ariella chuckled. "Great selfies, though!"

"I wish I could come back whenever I wanted," Yosef said, "but I have a feeling I won't ever see this again."

"Maybe not," Ariella replied. "But we have a door at the back of our library and now we know how to open it."

"If we can get back," Yosef reminded her. "Do you think the shed door will open now?"

"Only one way to find out," Ariella answered. "Come on. I'm hungry. If we get back in time, we can still have pizza."

"We can't say goodbye to Florence at a shed door, and then walk through it," Yosef said. "That'll look weird."

"True. Let's say goodbye to her now."

Florence was talking to the captain of a large

sailing boat. As they approached, they heard her asking about passage to Jamaica and saw her lower her head when he told her the cost.

Ariella took Florence's hands in hers. "We have so much to thank you for," she said. "But we need to go home now." Ariella hoped Florence would think she meant by boat, and not by time-travelling through a shed door that led to their school library two hundred years in the future.

"The honour has been mine," Florence answered, her eyes shining. "But Miss Ariella! You have lost your precious gold necklace!"

Ariella touched her throat and pretended to be surprised.

"No matter," Florence said firmly. "Elsie and I shall search high and low for it, and I shall post it to your forwarding address if I may have it."

Ariella smiled. "If you find it, I want you to sell it – to repay you for the clothes you bought us from your shop. You deserve to have enough savings to sail back and find your sister.

And I can guarantee that it wouldn't reach me by post, anyway."

"Oh, Miss Ariella, that is most generous. Are you certain?"

"Absolutely," Ariella replied. "Now, would you mind showing us the way back to Puddle Lane?"

Florence guided them the short but confusing way through the busy, narrow streets.

"This is it," Florence said as they turned the corner.

Ariella said, "Yes, here we are." She tugged Yosef's sleeve and whispered, "I can see the shed up ahead. Goodbye, wonderful Miss Florence!"

Yosef stopped walking. "Yes, goodbye, Miss Florence," he said. "I hope you find your sister."

"As do I," Florence said with a sad smile. "God be with you. I pray we meet again."

They waved goodbye and once Florence was out of sight, Ariella and Yosef walked towards the shed. The door was closed, but when Ariella turned the handle, it opened with ease.

"Ready?" Ariella asked.

Yosef did not seem as ready as she was. He took one last, loving look around, and said sadly, "Ready."

CHAPTER EIGHT
THE CABINET

Ariella opened the shed door and they walked through it into the library. Yosef glanced at the clock. It was only 4.10 pm: the exact time they'd left.

Ariella beamed. "I was worried there for a minute."

"Welcome back," said a voice behind them. "Been on your travels, I see." Miss Richie looked stern.

Ariella hung her head. "We were just curious. Are you cross with us?"

"A little," Miss Richie replied. "It can be dangerous. You should have asked me. But you've made it home so that's a relief. Clever you." Then, in a softer tone, she asked, "Where did you go?"

"We took the soap dish and went back to – I think it was the 1820s, I can't be sure," Yosef said. "We met Clara Conway when she was about ten."

"And saved her life," Ariella added. "Probably. The doctor had dirty hands and a disgusting apron."

"Gosh! Well done for that," Miss Richie said.

"And we met someone called Florence, who was incredibly kind," Yosef added.

"Hmm," Miss Richie said. She walked over to the biography section and picked out a thin book with a brown cover. "In this diary, written by Clara Conway, I'm sure she mentions a former slave called Florence who lived in their household." Miss Richie flicked through the pages. "Yes, here it is… *'In the year of the Lord 1830, my cousin's former housemaid,*

Miss Florence Woebegone, set sail to the Caribbean in search of her sister Mary, whom she hadn't seen since she was a child. The sisters were reunited, Florence purchased Mary's freedom, and they returned to London where they resided with us until they died. I suggested to my father that he change Florence's name to Freeman, and my father agreed. But Florence preferred to be known as Conway, and so she was.'"

Ariella's eyes stung. "Florence found Mary," she said with wobbly lips, and tried not to cry.

When Miss Richie walked off to put the book away, Yosef linked arms with his sister. "Nice one, Lella," he said. He couldn't quite manage the name 'Ariella' when he was little and sometimes still called her 'Lella' now.

Ariella bit her lip. "How will I explain to Grandma why I don't have the beautiful necklace she gave me anymore?" she whispered.

"We'll think of something," Yosef replied.

"Your brother will be here soon," Miss Richie said, coming back. "I'd imagine you're exhausted.

Time travel really takes it out of you – trust me, I know. Tell me all about it tomorrow. You can change out of those clothes in the toilet at the back and hang them in the small wardrobe. I have quite a collection from lots of different eras!" She pointed to the back door and her smile turned to a frown. "No one can know about this," she said, solemnly. "Ever."

Ariella and Yosef nodded, but then wondered whether shaking their heads was a better response, so they did that too.

Miss Richie laughed. "Good. And well done for using your initiative," she said. "Doctor Hurst's hands really were disgusting."

Ariella and Yosef were flabbergasted. "How do you know about that?" Ariella asked.

"I saw you both hiding under the blanket," Miss Richie replied with a grin. "So I came back to the library and slipped out of the door after you. I hid behind a carriage, watched from the Punch and Judy stand and waited outside the Conways' for you. Well, someone had to look out for you – I couldn't let you go walking around London in 1826 on your own now, could I?"

Ariella and Yosef smiled. "Is that why you wear these clothes now?" Ariella asked.

Miss Richie nodded. "Easier to blend in," she said. "Pink hair and colourful clothes stand out too much. And I'd run out of wardrobe space in no time!"

After the children had got changed, they went to check the cabinet. "The soap dish is here," Yosef said. And then he gasped. "Ariella! Look!"

Ariella stood beside him and scanned the shelves. Her gold chain and tree of life pendant sat on the middle shelf beside a label saying '**Circa 1870s**'.

"WHAT?" Ariella cried. "How on earth–? Why does it say 1870s?"

"They must have found it along with the Regency soap dish when they were building the new site," Miss Richie answered, unlocking the glass doors.

"But that makes no sense," Ariella stammered. She reached in and took it out, relieved. Her grandmother would have been so upset that she'd lost it, and her parents would have been, too. "But… if Florence sold it to pay for her passage to Jamaica, how could they find it here when they were excavating?"

Yosef shrugged and squinted at the objects with newfound interest. "Miss Richie, do each of these objects take you to this precise spot in different time periods?" he asked.

"Exactly," said Miss Richie.

"Have you been… everywhere?" he asked, wide-eyed.

"Nope. And there's a lot more to do. As you can see, when you go back and make changes, other things can turn up."

"Would we ever… be able to come with you?" Yosef asked hopefully.

"Maybe. I'm having terrible trouble with a vengeful Viking, and a cowherd in 1140 keeps losing his prize cow. See you tomorrow!"

On the way out of school, Ariella and Yosef stopped to look at the portrait of Clara Conway.

"I'm glad her leg recovered," Yosef said. "Now we know why she has that walking stick." He squinted hard at the portrait and then froze. "Hold on," he muttered. "What's… *that*?" He grabbed a nearby chair and stood on it to take a closer look. "No way!" he cried. "Lella, look at this!"

He climbed down and Ariella climbed up, saying, "What am I looking at?"

"Under her collar. There. Near the top of her dress."

Ariella gasped. "Is that... a gold chain?"

"And look down a bit. Isn't that the top half of a tree of life pendant?"

Ariella's eyes widened. "But–"

"Clara must have bought your necklace from Florence," Yosef said. "That would explain why it was found here in the 1870s–"

"Er... what are you doing?" the receptionist barked, coming in from the office at the back. "Get down from there immediately."

Yosef gave Ariella a hand down and mumbled, "Imagine all the things that have happened in this spot over thousands of years. Do you think we'll see any more of them?"

"Hope so," Ariella said.

They pulled the chair back, waved a warm goodbye to Clara, and with their big brother Daniel, stepped out on to Puddle Lane.

"I wonder what'll be here in years to come," Yosef said, standing still for a second. "Maybe there's another door somewhere in the school that'll take us into the future."

"Maybe," Ariella replied. "But right now, the only future I'm interested in is what pizza we're going to eat in half an hour. Let's go."

They walked through the London they knew best, gazing fondly at the glass skyscrapers, the cars and the buses, and the view of Tower Bridge in its rightful place above the Thames.

Now there was another reason they liked their school. But this one had to stay secret.

READING ZONE!

QUIZ TIME

Can you remember
the answers to these questions?

· Can you name the two London
landmarks near Puddle Lane School?

· Which object do Yosef and Ariella
take through the door?

· How do Yosef and Ariella work out
where they have travelled after
stepping through the door?

· What is the name of the cook
at the Conways' house?

· How did Miss Richie know that
the children had gone
through the door?

READING ZONE!

WHAT DO YOU THINK?

This book teaches the reader about some of the history of England and what it was like to live then. Do you think this is a good way to learn about history? Why/why not?

If it was possible, would you like to go on an adventure to a different period of history? Why/why not?

READING ZONE!

STORYTELLING TOOLKIT

We are introduced to Clara
early in the story, through
a portrait painting at the school.
The author uses the plaque
under the painting to give us
some details about the character.

At this point, we don't know how
important Clara is going to be
in the story. Do you think this is
a good way to give us background
information about the character
without giving the plot away?
Why/why not?

READING ZONE!

GET CREATIVE

There are other objects in the cabinet that would help Ariella and Yosef to go back in time (see page 17). Why not choose one of these objects and plan your own time travel story for Ariella and Yosef to go on? It could be to a different period of history.

Once you have planned your story, you could have a go at telling it to somebody or writing it down.

Look out for more books in the
BLOOMSBURY READERS SERIES

At the zoo, Maggie sees
a strange bird and takes one of its
beautiful silver feathers home.
Little does she know that this is the start
of a magical adventure in the moonlight...

Look out for more books in the
BLOOMSBURY READERS SERIES

From a mysterious traveller who leaves
an injured horse with a stranger, to a garden
plant that slowly creeps into a house during a
thunderstorm, this chilling collection of stories
will have readers jumping at bumps in the night.